For Ferd Monjo R.H.

For Theo M.B.

First published 1983 by Walker Books Ltd,
17-19 Hanway House,
Hanway Place, London W1P 9DL

First printed 1983
Printed and bound in Italy by Sagdos SpA

British Library Cataloguing in Publication Data
Hoban, Russell
Jim Frog. – (Ponders; v. 2)
I. Title II. Baynton, Martin
III. Series
823'.914 [J]   PZ7

ISBN 0-7445-0074-5

JIM FROG

RUSSELL HOBAN

Illustrated by
MARTIN BAYNTON

WALKER BOOKS
LONDON

Jim Frog was feeling a little low,
a little lonely, he had no hop in him,
he just dragged himself along.

At chorus practice he wouldn't sit up
straight on his lily pad, he just flopped
around. When everyone else croaked
'Jug-of-rum' he croaked 'Mug-of-jum'.

'Stop that!' everyone shouted. 'Why
can't you croak 'Jug-of-rum' like the
rest of us?'

'Nobody likes me,' said Jim.
'Everybody hates me.'

When it was snack time everybody
else got their nets and went out to catch
dragonflies. Jim couldn't be bothered, he
wasn't hungry, he couldn't find his net,
he didn't care. He took his harmonica out
of his pocket and played sad songs.

A head came out of the water, it
was Big John Turkle the snapper.

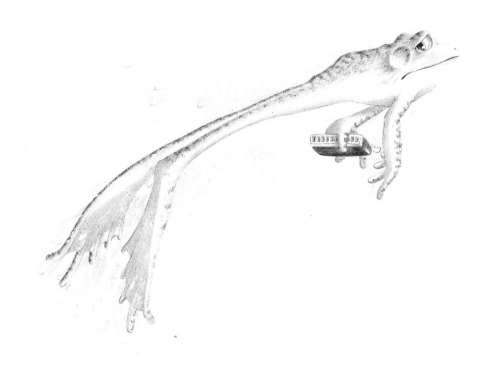

When Jim saw Big John he hopped
away fast.

'Nobody likes me,' said Big John
Turkle. 'Everybody hates me.'

Jim swam down to the other end of
the pond. He stuck his head up through
the duckweed and saw a damselfly nymph
crawling slowly up a cat-tail stem.

'Go ahead,' said the nymph. 'Eat me,
I don't care.'

'I'm not hungry,' said Jim.

'Everything's been so utterly rotten,'
said the nymph.

'I've been feeling a little low too,'
said Jim.

'Everything seems to be closing in on me,' said the nymph. 'I can scarcely breathe, I feel as if I'm going to jump out of my skin.'

'I feel a little lonely,' said Jim.

He was looking away from the damselfly nymph when he said that. When he looked back there was her empty skin split right down the back and the damselfly was out of it.

She looked altogether different, she waved her new wings dry then she flew away blue and glittering across the pond.

'How did she do that?' said Jim.
'I wonder if I can do it?' He climbed
onto a lily pad and tried to jump out of
his skin but his skin jumped with him.

'Ladies and gentlemen,' said a voice,
'your attention, please: Roland Waters
the pond-famous diving beetle will now
dive from a height of one inch into two
feet of water.'

The voice belonged to Roland
himself. 'Drum roll, please,' he said to
the cicada who was his partner.

The cicada did the drum roll and
Roland dived into the water.

'Did you see that?' he said to Jim.
'What a feat!'

'I thought it was two feet,' said Jim.

'What a joker you are,' said Roland.
'But it really was something, wasn't it?
I think everyone was impressed.'

Jim looked all around but he couldn't
see anyone but the cicada, who was
dozing in the sun.

'I suppose they were,' said Jim.

He felt like being alone so he went
down to the bottom of the pond and swam
into a hollow log. He took his harmonica
out of his pocket and began to play it.

Big John Turkle looked in. The hole
in the log was too narrow for him
so Jim was safe there.

'I can see the bubbles but I can't hear any music,' said Big John.

'Neither can I,' said Jim, 'but I know what I'm playing.'

'Is it happy or sad?' said Big John.

'Sad,' said Jim

'That's funny,' said Big John, 'the bubbles look happy.'

Jim went home. He noticed that he had a lot of hop in him. He thought of Roland Waters and he began to laugh. He was laughing and hopping, laughing and hopping all the way home.

When he got home his mother said, 'You look as if you've been having a pretty good day.'

'Actually it hasn't been bad,' said Jim, 'not bad at all.'